ticklish

This ⌃book belongs to

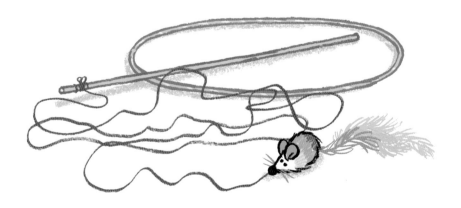

For Annie.

Henry Holt and Company, *Publishers since 1866*
Henry Holt® is a registered trademark of Macmillan Publishing Group, LLC
120 Broadway, New York, NY 10271
mackids.com

Library of Congress Control Number: 2019932416
ISBN 978-1-250-20667-1

Our books may be purchased in bulk for promotional, educational, or business use. Please contact your local bookseller or the Macmillan Corporate and Premium Sales Department at (800) 221-7945 ext. 5442 or by email at MacmillanSpecialMarkets@macmillan.com.

First published in the United Kingdom in 2018 by Oxford University Press
First American edition, 2019
Printed in China by Leo Paper Group, Gulao Town, Heshan, Guangdong Province
10 9 8 7 6 5 4 3 2 1

This book just stole my cat!

WITHDRAWN

Richard BYRNE

GODWINBOOKS

Henry Holt and Company · New York

Ben and his cat were
playing tickle and chase
across the page when . . .

. . . **something very odd happened.**

Ben's cat disappeared!

"Hello, Ben. You look like you've lost something!" said Bella.

"I've seen things go missing in here before," said Bella. "I'll take a peek."

But Bella disappeared, too.

Help quickly arrived to begin a search and rescue mission . . .

. . . then vanished.

I'll just have to do the rescuing myself! thought Ben.

But . . .

ACHOO!

Now everybody (except for a book-tickling fluffy mouse) was missing!

A little while later a
message appeared.

It read . . .

Dear reader,
Can you please help rescue us?
This book seems to sneeze when
it's tickled, so here are some
instruckshuns for you.

1. Wiggle your tickling fingers
to get them all warmed up.

2. TICKLE the
book in here...
...while counting tickly-one,
tickly-two, tickly-three!

3. Then turn the page...

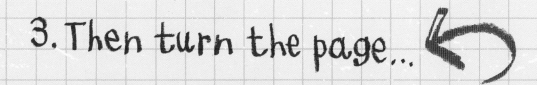

... and TICKLE here ...

... and
here ...

... and HERE!

Then please turn
the page again.

Everybody was rescued . . .

. . . and everything got back to normal.
(Well, almost everything!)

WHIRL
WHIRL

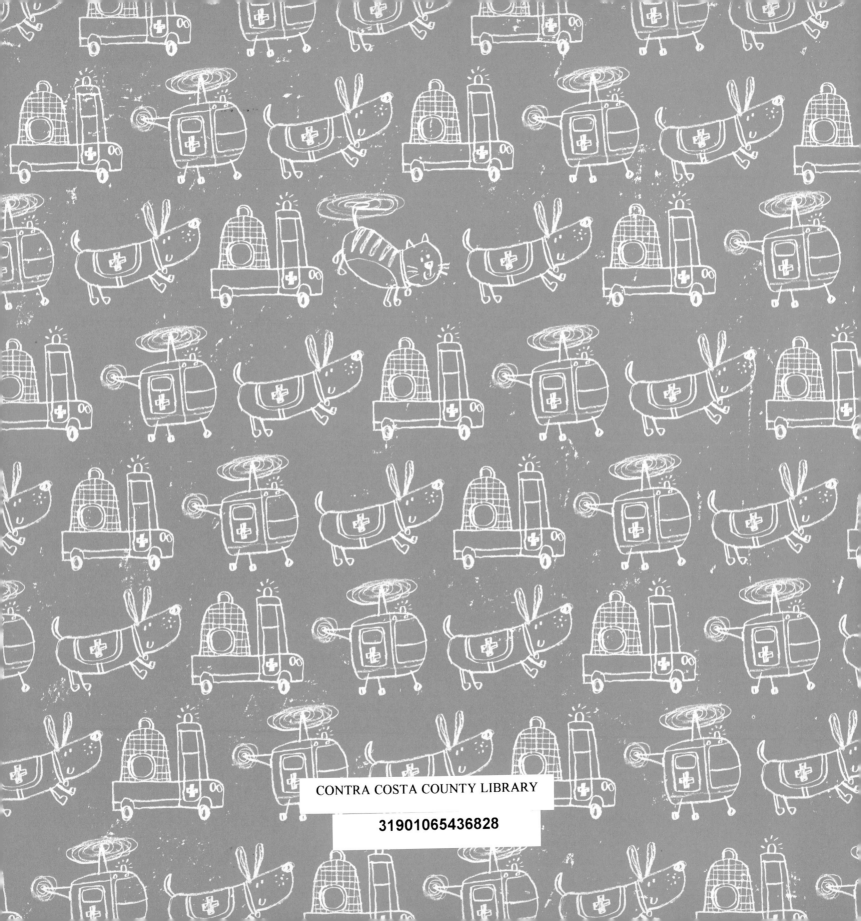